In the Spirit of Literacy
from Rosen Publishing

For further information: **rosenpublishing.com** or
contact your **NYS Digital Learning Representatives**:

Judi Dzikowski	Jane Lehmann
315-706-3350	**585-314-8599**
judid@rosenpub.com	**janel@rosenpub.com**

NYS Contract #: PC69954

THE SURPRISE PARTY RULES

BY MAX HOWARD

An imprint of Enslow Publishing

WEST **44** BOOKS™

Please visit our website, www.west44books.com.
For a free color catalog of all our high-quality books,
call toll free 1-800-398-2504.

Cataloging-in-Publication Data
Names: Howard, Max.
Title: The surprise party rules / Max Howard.
Description: New York : West 44, 2024. | Series: West 44 YA verse
Identifiers: ISBN 9781978596740 (pbk.) | ISBN 9781978596733
(library bound) | ISBN 9781978596757 (ebook)
Subjects: LCSH: American poetry--21st century. | Poetry, Modern--
21st century.| Poetry.
Classification: LCC PS584.H693 2024 | DDC 811.008'09282--dc23

First Edition

Published in 2024 by
Enslow Publishing LLC
2544 Clinton Street
Buffalo, NY 14224

Editor: Caitie McAneney
Designer: Leslie Taylor

Photo Credits: Cover (girl) LuckyN/Shutterstock.com, (checkmark)
OLYVIA/Shutterstock.com, (stars) keksik97/Shutterstock.com, (sign)
studiostoks/Shutterstock.com, (buttons) Andychi/Shutterstock.com.

Printed in the United States of America

CPSIA compliance information: Batch #CS24W44: For further information contact
Enslow Publishing LLC, New York, New York at 1-800-398-2504.

THE FIRST TIME I GOT FIRED

I worked at the hardware store
spring of junior year.

I made
one *tiny*
catapult.

Sent a few little
bolts flying. Cracked the
shop window.

So?

You only live once.

JULY 2

Fired. Again.
Bye-bye,
Pets Plus.

"What did you do?" my dad asks.

"Let the mice out," I say.

Mom looks up from frosting
cupcakes. "Oh, Ivy."

"I had to save them! How would
you like to be
snake food?"

"How would you like to go
without food?"
Dad starts in.

I tune him out.

Mom slips me a
pink cupcake.

AUGUST 10

I get hired at
Super Scoops Ice Cream Shop.

Mayor Payne owns it.
He comes in now and then.
Counts money.
Names flavors.

Mayor's Mint
Vote Vanilla
Cookies & Payne

When customers
come in,
he clips on a
red bow tie. A
red smile.
Scoops cones.

Calls me *kiddo*.

Because why would he
learn my name?

DAD DRIVES ME TO SUPER SCOOPS

We pass the new
hospital. Dad's
firm built it.

"See that?" Dad says.
"Now sick people have a
good place to go.
That's why we
work hard."

Dad frowns at me.
"Did you ask your
boss if it was OK to
dye your hair green?"

"Green? It's more teal," I say.

"Ivy, what's your plan for keeping this job?"

"When I find mice, I'll make
mice cream," I joke.

Dad rolls his cold blue eyes.
"You're almost eighteen.
When will you grow up?"

COWORKER

Little kids
mob Super Scoops after
T-ball games.

My coworker,
June, loves
them.

When kids
order toppings, she
spins around
yelling "Sprinkles!"
or "Whipped cream!" or
"Nuts! Nuts! I'm going nuts!"

MY DAD SAYS

there's something
off about
June.

I say there's
something
off about my
dad.

When he was my age, he
laid bricks. His hands
got blisters. Now he's a
vice president at the
company.

His life story is *work*.

It won't be mine.

I won't get blisters
scooping up
Chocolate Chip Mayor Dough.

I LEARN EVERYTHING ABOUT JUNE

June can
scoop three
cones a minute.

She's 50 and
lives in
Sunrise House.
It's a big house with
lots of porches.

People with
disabilities live there.

"My room has the
best view," June says.
"Blue river, blue sky, blue mountains."

June loves
blue. Blue Moon
ice cream. Blue shoes.
Blue nail polish.

So I dye my hair blue.

"Beautiful blue bob," June says.

MAYOR PAYNE

June feels
sorry for him
because he's
lactose intolerant.

I think he's just plain
intolerant.

He's all smiles and
bow ties for customers, though.

Politicians.
They're so fake.

His piggy-pink face is
printed on the
napkins. I
blow my nose on it.

FIRED—WITH A CHERRY ON TOP

I can't
open a jar of
cherries.

Maybe June can help?

I find her in the
back room with Mayor Payne.

"Idiot," he snaps.
"Moron."

"Don't talk to her
like that!" I say and—oops!

The lid
pops off the
cherries and—oops!

The juice flies out and
soaks his
shirt and—oops!

I'm fired.

MY BEST FRIEND GIGI

"The mayor fired you?
For cherry-bombing him?
We need revenge.
Let's switch
his soy milk
with real milk.
Give him a fart attack."

Gigi always knows just what to say.
She's funny, smart, and beautiful.
She has Z-shaped curls, but she
gets all As.

"I know what he'd
really hate.
To lose the
election," I say.

WET REVENGE

Gigi takes me to the
pool.

Oof.
My ex,
Jussie, is here.
They look so good with
wet hair. How can they
look so good and
think I'm
"too much"?

"Ivy, focus," Gigi says.
"We're not here for
love. We're here for revenge."

She
points to the
lifeguard.

"Alex Botero?"
I ask.

ALEX IN THE LIFEGUARD CHAIR

"Oh my God,"
Gigi says. "He's wearing
red trunks and a
red whistle. And *that's it.*"

"Gigi, focus," I say.
"We're not here for
love. We're here
for revenge."

She calls out, "Hey, Botero.
Heard you know about politics."

ALEX'S WHISTLE

Alex's sunglasses
flash. "What
do you need to
know about
politics?"

"How to make someone lose an
election," I say.

He blows his
whistle. Yells:
"Clear the pool. Everybody
out!"

He hops down
from his chair.

"How can I help?"

AT THE SNACK STAND

"So. What election?
Student council?" Alex asks.

"We want Mayor Payne to lose," I say.

Alex whistles.
"That's tough.
Payne is
powerful.
No one's even
running against him."

I buy him a Snickers.

"OK. I'm in," he says.

SENIOR YEAR

When school starts,
Alex, Gigi, and I ask
teachers to
run for mayor.

"We missed the
filing deadline.
But we can do a
write-in campaign.
Your team is ready,"
Alex argues.

Most teachers just say no.

But our government teacher
laughs.

"You couldn't
pay me enough to do that job,"
she hoots.

I TURN 18

Gigi dyes my hair
pink and takes me to the
movies. We walk into the
dark theater. The
lights snap on.

The crowd
yells: *Surprise!*

I jump, spilling my popcorn.

Everyone's here.
Even Jussie.

Red balloons
rain from the
ceiling. Sarah from
Yearbook bats them
at Jussie.

Ugh. She's clearly
in love with them.

Words drift across the
big screen:

IVY FOR MAYOR.

ALEX PUTS A SLIDE DECK ON THE BIG SCREEN

"Ivy can win.
Look at this graph,"
Alex says. "Hardly anyone
votes in local elections.
If people under 22
turn out to
vote November 7,
Ivy wins. Any
questions?"

Gus calls out,
"Which party?
Democrat or
Republican?"

"Ivy will represent
us." Jussie says it
like they like me.
Or at least . . . respect me?

"Sure," I say.
"I'll represent the . . .
Surprise Party."

Everyone laughs.

RAISING MONEY

Alex runs a hand
through his floppy
brown hair. "Maybe we
start with
online
fundraising.
Do a video.
You talking about
River Vale?"

"Boring," Gigi says.

"Yeah," I say. "That's not me."

But who am I, anyway?
I wonder.

"What about . . .
classic prankster?
That could be the
Surprise Party brand,"
Gigi says. "Vintage
vibes. Fun. We need
merch."

MERCH

Gigi and I look at
prank props online:

A plastic
ooze of
fake puke.

Whoopee cushions
that fart when someone
sits on them.

Fake snakes that
jump out of cans.

Hand buzzers
that zap whoever
shakes your
hand.

In the end,
we spend it all on
whoopee cushions.

PHOTO SHOOT

"I hate having my
picture taken," I say.

"Get over it," Alex barks.
"Politicians are
mostly just images in
people's minds."

"Sounds like being a
girl," Gigi says.
She uncaps her
red lipstick.

I squirm away.

Red looks great with
Gigi's warm brown skin tone.

But I'm so pale
lipstick makes me
look like a vampire.

GOING TO CITY HALL
WITH MY FRIENDS

Twenty of us
go to
City Hall.

Our footsteps ring
on the floor.

They echo on

stone walls

stone floors

stone columns.

Gigi looks at a map.
"This is the Main Hall.
The Council Chamber is that way."

THE COUNCIL CHAMBER

This room
feels like a church.

Instead of an
altar—a
big wraparound
desk.

Instead of a
cross—a flag.

Instead of priests in robes—
old people in suits.

No one laughs.
No one coughs.
No one whispers.

Is that what
power means?

Making people
afraid to talk?

THE FART-IN BEGINS

The Council members
look down
from their
altar/stage.

Mayor Payne
frowns. So does
his brother,
Councilman Payne.
They look just alike.

"Twins!" Gigi whispers.
"Creepy!"

"They have no idea what's coming,"
Alex says.

All of us
are armed with
whoopee cushions.

What we're about to do is
silly. It makes
no sense. But it's going to be a
BLAST.

THE MEETING STARTS

Mayor Payne
bangs the gavel

... and someone's
whoopee cushion
lets out a
squeaker.

It echoes off stone walls.

Mayor Payne stands up.
Scowls.

But he can't
do anything.

The room quiets.
He sits back down.

When his
butt touches his
chair, someone lets one
rip.

ORDER! ORDER!

Every time
Mayor Payne
yells "Order" and
bangs the gavel—

someone lets out another fart.

Bang! Fart!
Bang! Fart!
Bang! Fart-a-fart-fart-fart!

A tall, white-haired
councilwoman stands
up. She moves slow as a
snake uncoiling.

She shakes her wrinkled
finger. Sits down to a
fart explosion.

It's like an orchestra.
Instead of flutes,
farts. I'm
laughing so hard I
actually fart.

I'm definitely losing this election.
Might as well have fun doing it!

THE POLICE CHIEF

"What's going on?"
the police chief bellows.

The room falls silent.

The chief doesn't
touch her gun.

She doesn't have to.

The way she
stands reminds you
it's there.

"Free speech!"
Gus belches.

Sarah from Yearbook stands up.
"Nothing you do is worth a fart
until you do something about
climate change!"

SARAH MAY BE IN LOVE WITH MY EX

But her words
make me think.

Is running for mayor
about
more than just
revenge?

Half my
surprise party
came to the
fart-in.

They all care about the
climate.

Does the Surprise Party
actually stand for something?

We start getting
donations.

Not just from high school kids.
From random adults, too.

FLASH MOB

Fifty kids dress up as
Mayor Payne.

We wear spinning red
bow ties. Hand out
free ice cream
right in front of
his ice cream shop.

Script: *It's melting,*
Just like the ice caps.
Business as usual tastes great.

HALLOWEEN

I go as
Uncle Sam.

White beard.
Striped top hat.
Tall stilts.

"Is your homework done?" Dad asks.

"It never is," I say.
I'm so
tall in these
stilts, I can reach down and
pat his head.

Dad sighs.

"Does that
sigh mean
'you're lazy'
or 'you're ruining
your life?' I can't tell," I say, and
stilt out the door.

PEOPLE FOR CHANGE

"Ivy? Do you know a
group called
People for Change?" asks Alex.

"No," I say. "Why?"

"They just
donated $10,000."

"WHAT?" Gigi and I
jump to see Alex's screen.

It's real.
$10,000.

"Who are these people?" Gigi says.

"I don't know, but I like them," Alex says.

"What if they're
evil? We can't
keep their money," Gigi says.

"Agree," I say.
"We can't
keep the
money.
But maybe we
can give it away?"

HOW TO PLAN A
FOOD FIGHT

Rent:

Farmer's field
Trampolines
Bouncy Houses
Port-a-Potties
Buses (to take people to the field)

Buy:

First aid kits
Bottled water
Wrist bands ($20 to get in)
Mashed potatoes (to pack into balls)
Juice boxes (to squirt)
Pudding (to lob)
Lasagna (to fling)
Shaving cream and pie pans
(for pie attack)
Fruity Pebbles (to stick to everything)

NEWSPAPER HEADLINES

*RIVER VALE HOSTS STATE'S
LARGEST-EVER FOOD FIGHT*

*KIDS EARN $100,000 FROM
FOOD FIGHT,
GIVE IT ALL AWAY*

*NO MORE PIE-IN-THE-SKY
PROMISES: WOULD-BE TEEN
MAYOR RAISES COLD, HARD CASH*

*A FOOD FIGHT TO FIGHT HUNGER?
TEEN RAISES $100K*

*TEEN GIVES $100,000 TO LOCAL
FOOD BANK*

TV NEWS INTERVIEW

Gigi makes me
put on
red lipstick.
She rubs some
on my cheeks, too.
For color.

I feel like a vampire clown.

The reporter says,
"You raised $100,000.
Why aren't you
spending that
money on your
race? Don't you
want to win?"

"If you're hungry,
who cares who's
mayor?" I say. "I'd rather
feed people than win."

QUEEN GIGI

Gigi is the Spreadsheet Queen.

You have to be
very organized to
revolt.

Budgets.
Volunteers.
Supplies.
I thank her for all that work.

Gigi says, "No thanks needed.
This is my revenge, too."

"Revenge?"

"On my mom. Duh."

GIGI'S MOM

Gigi's mom,
Gretel Griffin,
runs the
School Board.

She's so blond
she owns wooden shoes.

(Being blond and
Dutch is her
thing).

So is banning books.

Her FaceChat page is
100 percent pics of
books with the
bad bits underlined.

It's like she
wants you to
read them.

GRIFFY PRINTS

Gigi's dad doesn't
wear wooden shoes.
He wears white
socks and red
Crocs. He runs
Griffy Prints and
hums while he
makes business cards.

When Gigi
complains about
banning books, her
dad smiles and says:

"Gigi, let your mom have her
hobby." His dimple is
just like Gigi's.

When Gigi's mom
tries to
destroy Gigi's social life,
Gigi's dad smiles and says:

"Gretel, let Gigi have her friends."

NOVEMBER

Our drone
hovers in the
crisp fall air.

The bell rings.
Kids rush out of
school.

The drone drops
copies of the
bad parts of
every book.

The drone drops
stickers, too.
Bright red.

They say:
Stop Reading!
These Words Are Banned!

STOP READING! THESE WORDS ARE BANNED!

The college
newspaper
does a story about the
stickers. Everyone
is banning their
textbooks. Telling
their profs: "I couldn't
study. My book
got banned.
See the
sticker?"

People ban parking signs and
pool rules.

Someone even
takes red paint and
bans the
mayor's billboard.

I don't *know* who did it.
But Sarah FaceChats a
pic of hands with
red paint
on them.

I know those hands.
They're Jussie's.

PEOPLE GET MAD

The local olds
rage on
BlockTalk and
FaceChat
about my
"disrespect."

Alex and I script a video.

"The real
disrespect is
censorship," I say.
"It's an insult to
young people's
intelligence. So
if I've insulted you with a
red sticker . . . good."

Alex posts the video.

Fifteen minutes later
I'm grounded.

GROUNDED ON ELECTION NIGHT

I'm 18
but "as long as I live under
this roof"
my parents can
ground me.

No phones.
No screens.
Plus I have to
pose for the
Perfect Family Photo Shoot.

(Mom needs pics for
InstaMom. It's how she gets
custom cake clients).

The three of us
wear red
sweaters and fake
smiles. We sip
cocoa for the camera.

I can barely swallow,
election night's
got me so nervous.

WINNING

At 10 p.m.,
50 members of
the Surprise Party
show up in my
yard.

They
bang pots and
pans. Drive
hundreds of
forks into my
lawn and
yell,

"You're the forkin' mayor!"

I wave from
my window
like Rapunzel.

When the local
news trucks show up,
the Surprise Party
TPs them.

I've never
laughed so hard.

GETTING SWORN IN

Suddenly, things get real.

Mom buys me a
blue pantsuit. I
want to dye my
hair to match it. But
Mom and I
settle on black.

We walk into the
Council Chamber.

I raise my right hand.
Say an oath.

The whole council stares me down.

I've upset adults before. I've been
grounded. Suspended. Fired.

But I've never seen such
mean looks. Even
my dad frowns.

"I hope you take this seriously,"
he says.

"Anyone for a swearing-in
sundae?" Mom asks.

I'M PROBABLY BANNED FROM SUPER SCOOPS

At the frozen yogurt shop,
June rings us up.
"June!" I say. "Do you work here now?"

"Yeah. The mayor fired me.
He said I voted for you.
But I didn't.
I voted for him."

"Sorry," I say.
"Um . . . do you still
live at Sunrise House?"

June smiles.
"Every morning the
sunrise gets more
beautiful."

ME, MOM, AND
THE PRINCIPAL

As mayor, I'll go to
work all day.

"Could I
study at night?
Do make-up work?" I ask
Principal Bruno.

His red mustache twitches.
"You're not a strong student, Ivy.
You need to be in class.
You want to graduate?"

"Yes."

"Then quit this
mayor mischief."

Mom stands up.
Knocks Dr. Bruno's
stapler off his desk
Snaps, "You should be
proud of her."

GRETEL GRIFFIN, SCHOOL BOARD PRESIDENT

Mom takes me to
Griffy Prints. She wants to
talk to Gigi's mom.

"Gretel, I voted for you.
You believe in parents' rights,"
Mom says.
"But Principal Bruno
won't listen to me
about Ivy. Will you
talk to him?"

Gretel gives me a look.
She slams the
paper cutter blade
like she's
chopping off my head.

"Let's make a deal," she purrs.

THE DEAL

"As mayor,
you're in charge of the
library. I want you to
set up a Parents' Board.
They get to
pick the books
for young readers," Gretel says.

"But that's censorship.
It goes against
everything I—"

"Do you want to graduate?
And be mayor?"
Gretel smiles as she slices.

"Yes."

"Then get me that Parents' Board.
Welcome to politics, sweetie."

FIRST DAY AS MAYOR

Alex's older brother,
Ben, owns a car
service.

On my first
day at work, he
picks us all up in a
long, black limo.

Ben drops Gigi and Alex at school.

Then he drives me to
City Hall. Drops me off.

I climb the big
stone steps alone. I wish
Alex and Gigi could
come with me.

MEETING MY TEAM

Weird.
I'm the boss.
I can fire people.

My staff is waiting in the
Main Hall.
They're all
old. All wearing
all black.

Black dresses. Black
suits. Black
skirts and tops.

Who knew
City Hall was so
Goth?

I sweat inside my blue pantsuit.
Say, "Hi, everyone."

MIKE BOONE

A tall, tall man
steps forward.

He moves slow as a
snake uncoiling.

His face is
freckled.
His smile is warm.
His green jacket is
too short. Somehow
that makes me feel
better.

"Morning, Mayor.
I'm Mike Boone,
your chief of
staff. I'll be
your right-hand
man. Let me show
you to your office."

MY OFFICE

Lemon-yellow walls.
River views.
Two couches.
Giant desk.
Giant spinny desk chair.

Mike thunks books
on my desk.
"The River Vale budget," he says.

Thunk. Another thick book.
"The city plan."

Thunk.
"The Staff Handbook."

Thunk. Thunk. Thunk. Thunk.
"The River Vale
legal codes.
Can I get you a coffee?"

I nod.

He leaves.

Finally,
I spin in the
spinny chair.

THE VETO

Mike brings me
paperwork.

"Here are
some bills for you
to sign."

I look over the
papers.

Freeze.

Someone bought
Sunrise House—
June's home.
They want to
tear it down.
Build fancy
waterfront apartments.

Where will June go?
Where will she see the sunrise?
Mike taps the paper.
"You can sign here."

"No. I can't," I
say, and rip the
papers into
confetti.

THE POLICE-AND-FIRE CHIEF

Mike says the
police chief is
also the fire chief.

"We combined the
roles a few years ago.
Her title is Safety
Chief. But we just
call her Chief Park.
She'll be here at ten."

But at 9:55 she calls.
Asks if I can meet her at the
jail instead.

THE JAIL

The vibes here make
my stomach
twist.

People are
crying. I can
hear them.

I want to let them out.
But this isn't
Pets Plus. This is
scary.

I wait in a
small room with a
big mirror.

Is this where they take
suspects?

THE CHIEF

Chief Park stares me down.
She's petite.
But scary.

My pantsuit
starts to itch.

"You want
blood on your
hands?" she barks.

"Is that . . . an offer?" I say.

"Answer me."

"No?" I say.

"Then resign. Quit.
Government isn't a
game.
People's lives are at
stake. Fires.
Heart attacks.
Murders."

MEETING THE LIBRARIAN

Lisa Lopes looks like a comic
book librarian.

Black dress.
Black boots.
Black bangs and black
cat-eye glasses.

"How's day one as our
first female mayor?" she asks.

I sigh. "The police
chief—"

"Don't let her
scare you.
You just keep doing
you."

CHECKING MY EMAIL

It's day one
but my inbox is
already full.

I skim.
Ignore the email from
Gretel Griffin, subject:
Parents' Library Board.

I can't deal with that right now.
I haven't even told Gigi.

I open a message from
Lisa the Librarian called

"New Mayor."

Right away,
I see I was
copied on this
email by mistake.

LIBRARY LISA'S EMAIL

To: All Staff
From: LibraryLisa@bookmail.com
Subject: NEW MAYOR

Principal Bruno says she's
"immature." Her
peers call her a
"freak."

This new
mayor needs to
quit.

Agree?

Show your support!

WEAR ALL
BLACK TO
WORK
EVERY
DAY
THIS WEEK.

GIGI READS THE EMAIL

I forward the
email to Gigi.
She writes back:

"They think
you're immature?

These are
grown
adults
doing a
dress-up week
to show how much
they hate someone?

City Hall is
worse than high
school."

FIRST COUNCIL MEETING

I try to learn
everyone's names.

Brinda Bahri—sharp chin.
Hot pink lipstick.

Ray Griffin—Gigi's fifth cousin.
(But she doesn't know him.)
Dark brown skin.
Long gray beard.
Bolo tie.

Ruth Boone —
white-haired
white woman. Currently
asleep.

Casey Payne—he's the
ex-mayor's twin.
Identical. Except
Casey has a lip mole.

He must *hate* me.

I miss my friends.
I bang the gavel.
Ms. Boone snorts awake.

IN OVER MY HEAD

I'm so lost,
I don't even know
when the meeting is over.

The sleeping lady has to
tell me to rap the desk.
End it.

Maybe I should end this
whole mayor thing, too.

I hate feeling clueless.

I hate the meanness.

I hate this itchy pantsuit.

As I'm leaving,
the sleeping lady
stops me.

THE SLEEPING COUNCILWOMAN SPEAKS

"I'm Ruth Boone.
I've been on this council
fifty years. Started as a
young chick of
thirty-five. I
didn't vote for you.
Why? Because you don't know
jack squat."

"Um, thanks?" I say.

"You've played video games?
Then you know
what to do. When you
beat a boss, you get a
treasure. A
gem. Maybe wisdom. Or a
jolt of magic.
Go. Fight some
battles. You'll be okay."

HOW TO WIN

Alex, Gigi, and I
eat takeout in
my office.

"Here's how you win,"
Alex says. "First,
learn the rules of the
game." He taps the
books
Mike Boone
left on my desk.

"It's better to know
the players," Gigi says.
"What do they
want? How
can you win them
over?"

AN ALL-NIGHTER IN THE MAYOR'S OFFICE

We study the
books on my desk.

Search for cheat codes.

Find the
City Hall
dress code.

"Weird! You
can't even wear
sandals," Alex says.

"How dare a
toe show its face in this
holy place?" Gigi cries.

"It's even stricter than
high school," Alex says.

That gives me an idea.

ALL STAFF EMAIL

To: All Staff; City Council
From: Mayor Ivy Sawyer
Subject: SPIRIT WEEK!

Hello Everyone,

This week is
SPIRIT WEEK at City Hall.

Show your CITY HALL PRIDE by
wearing the
SPIRIT WEEK color!

This year, the color is . . .

BLACK!

All of this week,
anyone wearing
black to work
will WIN a
free hug from me.

Sincerely,
Mayor Ivy

P.S. The dress code will no longer be
enforced.
Sandals for all!

THE LIBRARIAN

Gigi says,
"I found her
FaceChat.
@LibraryLisa
wants to
act cool. She's always
using this one hashtag.
#LibraryRebel."

"Gigi," I say,
"Your mom
asked me to
make a deal."

I explain about
Principal Bruno and the
Parents' Board.

Gigi picks up my
stapler. Throws it against the
wall. Bits of
metal fly out.

Then she says,
"Okay. We can work with that."

DAY TWO

I get to
City Hall
early, wearing an
all-black
sweat suit and
black sneakers.

I stand on the
steps. When people
walk in wearing
black, I say:

"Great outfit!
Way to show
City Hall
Pride!
Would you
like a hug?"

MY DAD STORMS INTO MY OFFICE

He shows me the newspaper headline:

TEEN MAYOR CANCELS
BUILDING PROJECT

I say, "*Teen* mayor? Instead of
just 'mayor'? That's
media bias—"

"My firm was
going to build
those apartments, Ivy.
And now my own
kid kills the deal?
My boss is so mad.
I could lose my
job. Fix this.
Sign the bill."

I don't make a joke.
I just say, "No."

CASEY PAYNE STORMS INTO MY OFFICE

At first, I
think he's the
ex-mayor.

Then I see his
lip mole.

Phew. It's the twin.

"I can't believe you
did this," he says.

"Let me guess," I say.
"The apartment building veto."

He makes a fist.
I flinch.

Is he
going to
punch me?

FISTS

"Don't leave me hanging," Casey says.
Wags his fist.

Oh.

I brush my knuckles against his.

"Way to go,
Mayor. I can't believe you
vetoed my twin
brother's pet
project. That
jerk was
set to make a
ton of cash.
Not anymore.
LOL."

"That wasn't why—" I start
 to say, but—

"I've got your back, kiddo,"
Casey says. "People for Change,
right? Just
watch out for that
Brinda Bahri.
Hot pink lipstick,
cold, cold
heart."

TOO MUCH IS GOING ON

People For Change?
They're the group that
donated $10,000 to
my campaign.

How does Casey know about
them? I wonder.

Was he the one
funding my
race?

Did he want to upset his
brother?

Does he want to be the next mayor?

Do I owe him something?

I can't think about it now.

I have a meeting.

THE LIBRARIAN LOOKS LIKE A BRIDE

She's wearing all white.
White dress.
White boots.
White purse.

"Sorry about my outfit," she
says. "I didn't see your
email until I got to work."

Liar, I think.

I read aloud from one of the
law books.

*"The mayor may start
new boards and task forces
when needed."*

I smile. "We need
a Library Parents' Board.
They can pick the books."

Lisa gasps. "You want to
ban books?"

BANNING BOOKS

"Lisa, you have a choice.
I can put
you in
charge of the
Parents' Board.
You can pick
board members who
won't ban anything.

Or, I can
put
Gretel Griffin
in charge."

Lisa's eyes bug.

"You don't have to like me, Lisa.
But I'm the mayor.
I deserve respect.

So. It's up to you.
Can we get along
like adults?"

She nods.

"Then spread the word," I say.
"I may be young.
But I don't play."

LUNCH WITH MIKE BOONE

Mike opens the
door of a
boxy white
street sweeper.

"Hop in," he says.

We drive slowly.
The spinning brushes
whisk up
autumn leaves.

We pass the
school. Kids are
eating lunch on the
lawn. I stick
my head out the
window. Wave.
Everyone claps.
It's like I'm in a
parade.

STREET SWEEPER

"What's the point of a
street sweeper?" I ask.

"When it rains,
whatever's on the
street washes into the
watershed. That can
be road salt. Oil
from cars. Plastic
trash. Street sweepers
protect the water."

"We should put that on a
T-shirt," I say. "Street
sweepers are cute and
good for the planet."

LUNCH

We drive the street sweeper
up to
Blue Ridge Park.

We find Ruth Boone
cooking hot dogs on a grill.

From up here,
River Vale
looks tiny.
The river
travels as far as I can see.
It yawns
into lakes.
Twists into
skinny
creeks.

"Did you know the river is
thirty *million*
years old?" I say.

Mike pats Ruth's
arm. "That's even
older than you, Mom."

"What? Ruth is your
mom?" I say.

THAT'S RICH

Mike brings me 500 street sweeper
T-shirts.

"As requested," he says.

I've got to be
careful what I
say around him.

He gives me
my paycheck, too.

I go wild online,
buying presents.

Red velvet Jimmy Choos for
Gigi. For Alex, silver high-tops.
Limited edition.

I'll save the next check.

THE PARENTS' BOARD

The news does a
story about the
new Parents' Board.

Five minutes later,
Mom texts.

Principal Bruno had a
change of heart.
I can study at night.

I don't hear a peep from
Gretel Griffin.

But I picture her
working the
slicer.

MY DAD'S LETTER IN THE NEWSPAPER

*Mayor Sawyer is
my daughter.
I love her.*

*But she's a kid.
That's why I didn't vote for her.*

*Last week, she shut down a
great building project.
She didn't think about
the impact.*

*As a parent, you
hate to ask others
to clean up your kid's mess.*

*But I'm asking the City Council.
Please. Vote down Ivy's veto.*

ANGRY PASTA

I try to do
homework while
Mom chops carrots.
Her knife
sounds angry.

Dad walks in. She
snaps, "I saw what you
wrote. How *could* you?"

Dad says, "No
one reads the
paper. Besides. My
boss made me.
It's no big deal."

The pasta
water boils
over. It
hisses on the stove.

I get up.
Walk to City Hall.
It's more peaceful than my kitchen.

GIGI DYES MY HAIR IN MY OFFICE BATHROOM

"I can't believe
your dad went to the
media," Gigi says.

"I can," I say with a shrug.
"My dad only loves me
when I do what he
wants."

Gigi paints bleach on my
roots. It feels soothing.

"We need to get
control of the media story," Alex says.

"Alex and I will take
care of everything.
You just sit tight, Ivy," Gigi says.

Mom stops by
with cookies.
"Mayor Macaroons, anyone?"

MOM FEEDS ME COOKIES AND A SOB STORY

"Your dad's past taught him
life is rough. There's only
one way to be safe.
You need to shut up.
Work hard. Follow
rules. Obey
powerful people.
He's trying to protect
you. In his own way."

The cookies are InstaMom-perfect.
But they taste like chalk dust to me.

"I don't need
protection. I need
respect," I say.
"Now I have to go
wash bleach out of my hair."

LIMOS

At 6 p.m.,
long black
limos crowd
Main Street.

The limos stop in front of
City Hall.

They're all from
Alex's brother's company.

Alex and Gigi hold signs.

They say:

Stuck in Traffic?
Thank your
local chapter of
Big Money.

BIG MONEY

City Hall is
packed with kids.

"What is this,
fart club again?"
Ray Griffin mutters.

But today,
there are no
whoopie cushions.

There are ball gowns.
Tuxes. Top hats.

My Surprise Party team is
all dressed up.

They're carrying signs, too.

Vote Down the Veto!

Give me River Views—
or Give Me Death!

We're Big Money and We Always Win.

HOT IN A TUX

Jussie looks hot in a
tux. Our eyes meet.
Their eyes are
so black they're almost
blue-violet. And
Jussie has this
way of leaning
up against a wall...

They tip their top
hat. Mouth,
Nice purple hair.

I look away.

Mayors
never blush.

THE COUNCIL VOTES

They undo my
veto. Even Ruth
votes against me.

Only Casey Payne supports me.
Not because he thinks I'm right.
Because he hates his brother.

Sunrise House will be torn down.

My dad wins after all.

AFTER THE MEETING

Ruth touches my
arm.

I flinch.

"You fought a good
fight," she says.

"Don't you care about the
people at
Sunrise House?" I say.

"They'll find
another place," she says.

"Not with river views," I say.

"Think big picture," Ruth says.
"Do you know what
fancy apartments mean?
Tax dollars. That's
money you can
use to help folks."

"So we should just
sell out?" I say.

"Sometimes," Ruth says.

WATCHING THE 10 O'CLOCK NEWS WITH ALEX

A reporter interviews
Jussie. Their top
hat is askew.
It covers one
eye. How do they
always look
so good?

"We represent
Big Money," Jussie says.
"We demand you
tear down
Sunrise House.
Build something for
us. Who cares about the
folks that live there?
We want those
river views!"

My inbox keeps dinging.

"Is that the
sweet sound of
public outcry?" Alex asks.

"People are mad," I say.
"They want to
save Sunrise House."

TAKE YOUR CHILD TO WORK DAY

When I was 10,
Dad took me to
a job site.

A black wrecking ball
swung through a
blue sky.

It smashed into a
concrete wall.

The earth shook.
My heart jumped.
I dropped my
Sprite. It
fizzed over my
shoes. Dad didn't
even care.

"This is the best day,"
I told him.

"You're the best daughter," he said.

How quickly things change.

TAKE YOUR PARENT TO WORK DAY

I make a FaceChat video.
Say:

"Take your
child to work
day began in 1993.

The goal?
Teach kids about the work world.

By now, many of those
kids have their own jobs.

Their parents
don't always know
what their kids'
lives are like.

Today, I declare
December 10th

Take Your Parent To
Work Day at
City Hall."

I hit "post."
Tag Dad.

RUTH TAKES ME TO LUNCH

"Dress up,
toots. We're
going somewhere nice,"
she says.

Ruth's old car
rattles. Stinky smoke
puffs out the
back. We
roll up to the
Country Club
smelling like
rotten eggs.

"Got any
whoopee cushions?
Or do I need to
pat you down?"
Ruth asks.

"We're good," I say.

Ruth nods at the
guard.

The gate swings open.

THE COUNTRY CLUB DINING ROOM

Candlelight. Thick
rugs. Heavy
drapes. Blurry old
paintings.

And my dad's boss.

Ada Vine.
She's the queen of
River Vale.

She looks like a
Ferrari sounds.

"Why are we here?"
I ask.

"No need to
whisper. You're the
Mayor of River Vale.
This is your
hunting grounds,"
Ruth says.

LUNCH WITH ADA VINE

Ada shakes my hand.
"Hello, Mayor.
I'm Ada. But
you can call me
Big Money.
I *know* you can
because
that's what you
do call me."

"We call you
wrecking ball, too,"
I say. "Do prefer that?"

Ada snorts.

Ruth beams. "I knew
you two gals would get
along. Who wants
shrimp cocktail?"

Ruth gets us laughing.
Then Ada tells her story.

ADA'S STORY

"You and I started in the same spot—
scooping ice cream.
But I was sick of it.

So I called
up this
CEO. Lied.
Said I was
this big banker.

We set up a golf
game. I get a hole in
one. Ah-ha.
Now he wants
golf tips.
Stock tips.
Takes him weeks to
figure out I'm just
an ice cream girl.
When he does, he
gives me a job.

That was twenty years ago.
Want to see a
picture of my boat?"

EATING RAMEN AT MY OFFICE

I tell Alex and Gigi
about Ada. "I almost
liked her," I say.

"Good. Ada's a powerful
ally," Alex says.

I slurp noodles. "Power isn't
everything."

"How can you do
good without
power?" Alex asks.

"How can you
be good *with* power?"
Gigi taunts.

She sticks her
tongue out at him.

His eyes go black.

Oh, I realize.
Alex likes Gigi.

PARENTS' DAY

I look out the
window.

An older woman
pushes a
red walker toward
City Hall.

I run out.
Salt the sidewalk for her.

She smiles a
hot pink
smile.

I say, "I know that
lipstick. You must be
Councilwoman Bahri's
mom."

"This shade's called
Party Pink," Brinda's mom says.
"I've worn it
since Mother's Day
1985. But they don't make it
anymore. I'm down to my
last tube."

GOOD EMAIL

My inbox is full of stuff like:

"Can we do Parents' Day every year?"

"My dad rode in the
fire truck!"

Brinda writes,
"Thanks for helping my mom."

Even the chief smiled at me today.

Parents' Day was a hit.
I wish my dad had come.

He said Ada made him
go to a job site.

Should I believe him?

THE COUNCIL MEETING

Ruth says, "We need to
save Sunrise House.
People are so
mad about it."

Ray says,
"They're so mad,
you'd think
we were
raising parking fees."

Ruth laughs. "Don't
even say those
words. *Parking fees.*
We'll all lose our seats."

Brinda rolls her eyes.
"That anger?
It's fake news.
The mayor's stirring it up."

Ouch.
Casey was right about her.
Hot pink lips; cold, cold heart.

But we get the votes.
We save Sunrise House.

SNOWSTORM CLEANUP

Mike teaches me to
drive a snowplow.

Waves of snow
whoosh up around us.
"It's like surfing," I say.

I learn how to
pile up snow
using a skid steer, too.

It's a forklift-sized
digger, good in
tight spaces.

We plow the
alley behind the
Froyo place.

"Hey Mike," I say. "How about
I buy us a treat?"

FROYO

June cashes me out.

"How's Sunrise House?"
I ask.

June rolls her eyes.
"Bad. I was
going to move to a
horse ranch.
But not anymore."

I drop Mike's key lime yogurt.
Splat.

Oh, no.

Was that
big fight for Sunrise House
all for
nothing?

Why didn't I
ask what the Sunrise House
residents wanted?
I wanted to protect them.
But did I disrespect them?

THE BOOK BOAT

There's a
boat in the
library lobby.

It's a little
fishing boat with
an outboard motor.

A sign says:
"Ahoy! The Anti-
Censor-SHIP."

"That's a *ferry* good boat pun," I say.

Lisa says,
"The Parents' Board
set this up. The
Parents' Board was a great
idea, Ivy.
I chose a few cool
people.
Now *they* deal with the
complaints."

SARAH'S FACECHAT VIDEO

Sarah from Yearbook makes a
FaceChat video:

Sarah's nose ring
sparkles when she
scowls. "Ivy Sawyer ran on
change. But
what has she done?
Sure, City Hall now
flies a rainbow flag.
So what? We want
real action."

What do you want me to do?
I think.
I'm not a king.

"Ivy's so fake.
See how often she
changes her hair?
That's how often she
changes her mind,"
Sarah says.

WINTER FORMAL

No one asked me to the
dance. Not even
Alex and Gigi.
(They went *together*.)

I stay in my office.
Work.

Sarah and Jussie post kiss pics.

I call Gigi. She answers,
laughing.
"My new red velvet heels
gave me blisters. Now
Alex has to
carry me everywhere."

I want to yell,
"My *heart* has a blister!"
but no one cares.

ALONE IN CITY HALL

I wander into the
Main Hall.
Moonlight
shines white on
the marble steps.

I sit down.
Let the cold
stone chill me out.

Sarah's right.
I am a
fake.

I pranked my
way here.

And now
I don't know
what to do.

Sunrise House
took so much
work. And
was it even the
right thing to
do?

I USED TO GIVE GREAT CHRISTMAS PRESENTS

Last year I
gave Gigi a
spoon. Her
favorite singer once
used it to stir tea.

This year I'm
shopping at the
24-hour drugstore
on Christmas Eve.

It's picked over.

I find Party Pink lipstick in the
discount bin.

But that's it.

Brinda will get lipstick.
For everyone else, it's
street sweeper T-shirts.

CHRISTMAS MORNING

I shouldn't text Jussie.

But it's Christmas.

"Ivy, put down your
phone. We're
doing presents,"
Mom says.

Dad doesn't
say anything.
He's pretending we're
perfect.

I text Jussie.

Merry Christmas!!!
PLEASE.
Go make out with
Sarah. Anything to
keep her off
FaceChat.

Mom hands me a big
red box.

THE RED BOX

I open the lid.

A cloud-white puppy
leaps into
my arms.

Holding her, a
sunlight feeling
fills my chest.

"Do you love her?"
Mom asks from
behind her phone.
She's making a
reaction video for
InstaMom.

Dad stands behind
Mom. He's smiling
a not-fake smile.

The puppy snuggles close.
I close my eyes.
"Yes."

HOLIDAY GREETINGS

I mail the lipstick to
Brinda. My card says:
"Happy New Year to
you and your mom!"

I *do* want them to have a good
New Year.

But also I want to win
Brinda over.
How fake am I?

I need Brinda's vote to
change things.

And I need to
change things to
shut Sarah up.

LEAVING GUS'S NEW YEAR'S EVE PARTY EARLY

Everyone's toasting
with fizzy pink wine.

"Bye y'all. I've got to
go," I say. "Don't
want to get busted
for underage drinking."

"Think of the headlines,"
Gigi shudders.

"The chief would love
throwing me in jail,"
I say.

I walk to City Hall alone.

I should do homework, anyway.
I'm behind.

Jussie texts:

You left.

JUSSIE'S TEXT

You left?

That's it?

Nothing for days and then
You left? Just a
statement of
fact?
I won't reply.

No.

Not

                    yet.

NO SHELTER

A man is
lying on the
City Hall steps.

Oh, no.
Is he dead?

His frosty
breath glows in the
moonlight.

Phew. He's alive.

"Happy New Year," I say.

"You the teen mayor?" he asks.
"The shelter is full.
It's freezing.
Where am I
supposed to sleep?"

I shrug.
"There's a couch in my office."

THIS IS ONLY A LITTLE UNSAFE

The police station
is across the
street. They
keep an eye on
City Hall.

This is only a little
unsafe. Right?

"Name's Ken," the man says.
"Want a violet mint?"

I take one.
"My grandpa loves these."

Ken sleeps on the couch.

I study the budget.
Fall asleep on my desk.

NEW YEAR'S DAY

Ken and I drink
office coffee.

When Mike gets in,
I pour him a cup.
"I found some
room in the
budget. Maybe
we could expand
the shelter?"

"Why not help
people rent
homes instead?" Ken says.

"I'll look into it.
Make a report,"
Mike says.

"Where do I sleep till then?"
Ken asks.

These are some tough questions.

TAKING MY PUPPY
TO WORK

I set up
cots in the
Main Hall.

People need a place to
sleep. Why not here?

My puppy runs
circles at my feet.

I unroll a sleeping bag.

Brinda rolls it back up.

"People can't
sleep here.
What if something
happens? We'll
get sued."

"We have insurance," I say.

"Mayor!"
Brinda snaps her fingers at me.

My puppy is peeing on the floor.

Oops.

TOO FAR

Gigi finds
volunteers. They
work nights at
City Hall. Even
Sarah signs up.

It's not all
cocoa and
pj's. Chief Park
does a
Narcan
training and
a safety demo.

Alex checks the
buzz on social.

"Are people mad?" I ask.

"Some are," he says.
"You're making it clear that
everyone belongs."

WINTER CAMPING

Protesters
set up
tents on
my front
lawn. Their
leader?

Gigi's mom.

She stomps around in
pink snow pants.
Plants signs in the snow.

Save City Hall!
Taxpayers for Common Sense!

A woman pounds on our
front door. Yells:
"Like it when we sleep on
your property?"

A man pounds on the
back door. Squeals:
"Little piggies, let me in!"

GOING BANANAS

I hold my puppy.
She's shaking.
There's shouting
outside and Mom
is slamming
cupboard doors, too.

"I'm sorry,
Mom. It's my
fault," I say.

Mom says, "I'm not mad at
you, Ivy. Get my
phone. Film me.
InstaMom is about to
go bananas."

Mom puts the kettle on.

"What are you doing?" I ask.

"Serving them
cocoa."

RIVER VALE'S FIRST DOG

I put my puppy in a
pet sling. Take her to
visit a third grade class.

"Do you want to help name her?" I ask.

The kids yell names.

Fluffbutt.
Sugarbutt. "No butts,"
the teacher says.

Pizza
Big Pizza!
Tiny Pizza!
Tiny Green Pizza!

The whole city votes online.

Tiny Green Pizza wins.
But I call her
"Pizza" for short.

A GOOD WEEK

My puppy
learns
her name—
Pizza.

A blizzard hits.
It blows the tents
right off my lawn.

Mike gives me a plan. It's for a
Rent Help program.

Council passes it quickly.

Maybe because the
people who live at
City Hall
are there,
watching.

FEBRUARY

We get another
foot of snow.

It's the snowiest winter on record.

Mike has bad news.
"Ted took a skid steer out
to help clear snow.
It stalled on the train
tracks. Then he heard the
train coming."

"Is he okay?" I ask.

"He got out in time.
But the skid steer—it's
toast."

STEERING INTO A SKID

"We have to
buy a new skid steer,"
Mike says. "We
can't clear
alleys without it.
But we don't
have the money.
Unless we
cancel the
Rent Help program."

"What about insurance?" I ask.

It gets quiet.

Pizza's toenails
click across the floor.

"I didn't make the payments,"
Mike says. "We don't have insurance
for that."

UNSAFE

My phone pings.
A text from
Jussie.

I don't even read it.

"Mike,
why didn't you make the
payments?" I ask.

"There's a problem.
I thought I could fix it before
anyone noticed—"

"What kind of a problem?"

"It's my problem.
Gambling."

Outside, the
winter wind
screams. My heart
screams, too.

STEALING

Mike stole from the
city.

Jokes can't fix this.
Puppies can't fix this.
Costumes and food fights
can't fix this.

Mike looks weak.
I help him onto the
couch. Pizza
hops up.
Licks his face.

I try to keep it together.
"I'm sorry, Mike.
You know what I have to do."

He nods.

I call Chief Park.

MIKE GETS ARRESTED

Two officers
lead Mike away.
Mike looks back at me.

"Please don't tell my
mom. Not till you
have to."

Pizza
sits on top
of my feet.

Chief Park
gives me a tissue.

That's how I
figure out

I'm
crying.

CHIEF PARK

The chief and I
stare out the
window. We watch
Mike go
into the jail.

"I told you to quit.
You should've listened,"
Chief Park says to me.
"I sensed this could happen."

I think back.
"So, that day at the
jail . . . you acted
so scary. Were you
trying to warn me?"

"Yes," she says.

"Why? You don't even like me."

THE WARNING

"Being a woman
leader is hard,"
Chief Park says.
"It's even harder
if you look young.
I'm a good police
chief. I've won awards.
But people treat me like
a child because I'm a
small Asian woman.
We need strong
women to lead.
Not . . . fart around.
That sets us all back."

She looks at me.
"You okay?"

"No," I say. "I need a new
skid steer."

DAD

I storm into Dad's office for a change.

"Ivy," he says, "I'm
at work."

"This is business," I say.
"Ada and I
made a deal."

"Ivy—"

"I'm giving her the
key to the city," I say.
"So give me the key to the
skid steer."

THE COUNCIL MEETING

Ruth's chair is empty.

I'm so worried,
I don't even care that
Sarah and Jussie show up
holding hands.

Sarah goes to the
mic. Says:

"Why did
this mayor let
Ada Vine Construction
put up a billboard
in the park? How
corrupt."

I don't care.
All I can think about is
Ruth. Is she okay?

THE HEADLINES

Chief of Staff Steals City Funds

City Broke; Teen Mayor's Staff Gambled It All Away

"Mayor Must Quit," says School Board Prez

Teen Mayor Caught in Scandal

500 People Sign a Petition to Recall Teen Mayor

"Recall Ivy" Petition Signed by 1,000

Ex-Mayor Payne Ready to "Step In"

WORSE NEWS

Ruth Boone had a
stroke. Her
daughter Deb—Mike's
sister—calls me.

"She's lost her
speech," Deb says.
"She can't walk.
We're sending her to
Park Pines."

"The nursing home?"

"Rehab," Deb says.
"She can
get treatment
there. Strengthen her
muscles. Heal."

MEETING DAD
FOR COFFEE

He shows up
wearing the
street sweeper T-shirt.

My Christmas gift to him.

His lips twist.
Like he's waiting
for words.
"I thought you'd quit
when things got hard.
You didn't.
I see it now. You're
building something."

He opens his
briefcase. Hands me a
brick. It's warm and
heavy in my palm. "I'll
try to build you up
from now on, okay?"

THE LETTER

A company
called
Life Water
wants to
buy River Vale's water.

They'll
run our
water treatment plant.

Sell the water
back to us.

How can you even
do that—own
all the water
under the ground?

Doesn't it belong to
everyone? Water
moves. Flows.
Owning it
is like
owning
air.

They're offering a lot of money.

BRINDA WITHOUT LIPSTICK

Brinda stops by.
She's not wearing
Party Pink lipstick.

She looks
shaky without it.
"At our
next meeting,
we are going
to vote to ask
you to resign.
I wanted to
let you know."

My phone pings.
It's Jussie.

I feel so shaky and
I delete it,
without looking,
by mistake.

PARK PINES
NURSING HOME

"My Dutch grandma lives in
Park Pines," Gigi says.
She trims my hair with
office scissors.

"Frida? Who makes the
waffle cookies?" I ask.
"Does she like it there?"

"No. But she likes the creek
nearby. She can fish. Hold still."
Gigi cuts my bangs.

Faded purple hair falls.

"There. Now I can see," I say.

"Your roots are
growing out."

"I have a meeting," I say.
"No time for hair dye."

RUTH

Ruth's chair is the
color of an old
Band-Aid. Her
blanket is, too.

"I'm sorry," I say.
"About Mike.
About
everything."

Her lips twist.
She can't find words.

"You don't have to talk," I say.

She holds out her hand.

I set a hand buzzer in it.

"Now you can prank the nurse," I say.

Ruth laughs with her eyes.

WATER

Ruth taps
my hand.

Her lips twist.

We wait for the
words.

"Water," she says.

"Thirsty?"

She shakes her head no.

Stamps her
good foot. "Underwear."

"Underwater?" I guess.

She nods.
Stamps. "No," she
says. "Don't."

I don't know what
she means. But I
promise to visit again.

PITY TACOS

Alex and Gigi
take me out to eat.

"You've got to
send all the city
records to an
accountant. An
outsider. Get
fresh eyes on it,"
Gigi says. She knows.
She does
Quickbooks at the
print shop.

"Okay," I say.
I scoop salsa onto a
chip. "I've moved
money around.
Paid our insurance.
But what
happens when I
can't pay the bills?"

FLINT

Alex says,

"In 2014, Flint,
Michigan,
ran out of money.

That meant the
governor could
get rid of the mayor.

Put someone else in.
Someone who'd
make hard cuts.
Pay the bills.

The new manager
came in.
Cut corners.
They wound up
with lead in their
water. Kids got
poisoned."

SARAH POSTS A VIDEO

"Ivy
Sawyer must
resign. The
youth of River Vale
deserve a
real leader.
Not a fake.
That's why
I am running
to be the next
Mayor of River Vale."

I laugh until I
snort.

Good luck, I think.
You'll need it.

Jussie texts:

*Sorry about
Sarah. I tried to
tell you, but
you didn't text me back . . .
XO*

HOW BAD IS IT?

I get
an outside
firm to
review the books.

"If you
make it through
this year, you'll be okay,"
the accountant says.

"Great," I say.

"But you're not
going to make it
through this year.
Not without a
lot of extra
money coming in."

I TEXT JUSSIE

Don't be sorry.

*If River Vale can't pay its
bills, we won't
HAVE a mayor.*

*The state will
take over.*

*They'll sell our water to
a private company.*

*So go pour yourself a glass
while it's still free.*

Drink up, buttercup.

XO

VISITING RUTH

She shakes my hand.

I should be prepared.
But I'm not—
She *zaps* me with the
hand buzzer!

I jump.
She laughs.

"The council is going
to ask me to resign, I say.

Ruth's lips
twist:
"Squat."

"Do you mean . . .
jack squat?"

She nods, a
gleam in her eye.

I get it.
They can ask me
to quit. But they
can't make me.

ST. PATRICK'S DAY

My feet are
wet and cold.

It's been rain and
sleet and
snow all week.

The council votes.

They ask me to
resign. Only
Casey has my
back.

I can't feel my
toes.

I can't feel anything.

GIGI IS CRYING

At first I think it's
about the vote.
It's not.

"Everyone's hearing back from
colleges. What if
Alex gets into
State and I don't?"

"Then we'll
move to Paris," I say.
"The state will
take over River
Vale. And I've
been saving money.
Why not?"

LIFE WATERS

I read about Life Waters
online.

Their
office tower in Florida has a
moat.

I zoom in.

Signs say
"NO WADING.
ALLIGATORS."

Not creepy.
Not creepy at all.

A VIDEO CHAT WITH LIFE WATERS

I talk with CEO
Brooke Lake.

That's her real name.

"Alright-y, Ivy!" she
says. "We know
you're in a
jam. But
we can fix it.
We'll run
your water plant
for you.
And we'll give you a
nice lump
sum. You
can buy those combat
tanks you want!"

"Tanks?"

She checks her notes.

"Sorry. That's another
mayor. *You*
want to buy a
wind farm."

BROOKE TALKS WATER

"What about
drinking water?"

Brooke smiles.
"No changes.
People will
turn on the
taps. Water will
come out.
Their bills will come from us.
That's all."

"Will it cost the same?" I ask.

Brooke runs a
hand through her
gelled hair.
"Of course!
For now."

THE DEAL

"I'll email you
the contract,"
Brooke says.

"But act fast, Mayor.
When you run out of
cash, the
state takes over.

We can make a
deal with them.

Like it or not,
Life Waters
will own your water.

So here's your choice,
Mayor:
Wind farm or
no wind farm?
Job or no job?
Alright-y?"

THE WORST GIFT BASKET

Life Waters
sends me a
gift basket.

"There's nothing in
it," Gigi says.
"No chips.
No nuts.
Just bottles of water."

"And a note," I say.
"It says: Enjoy these fine
waters
from around the
world!"

"Wait," Gigi says.
"Do they
want to
bottle our
water and
sell it?"

AT BLUE RIDGE PARK

I look down at
the river. It's
swollen with
snowmelt and
racing.

The river is
millions of
years old.
It's known
floods. And
droughts. And
people worse than Mike.

But Mike did
what he did. And
now . . .
will the river
be slurped up in
Life Water's straw?

MIKE'S OUT ON BAIL

He meets me on top of
the ridge.
His street sweeper T-shirt has
red jelly on it.

"Ivy, I'm so sorry—"

"Life Waters wants to
buy our water.
We have no money.
What do I do?" I say.

"I'm sorry,"
Mike says.
"I can't help you.
I can't even help myself."

Walking back to my
car, it starts to rain.

STILL RAINING

I wake up to
a message
from the
Streets Team.

Ice is clogging the
storm drains.

Everyone needs to
go and clear it.

If they don't,
the city will flood.

I shove my
messy hair into a
ponytail. Go out in pj's and
rain boots.

Hack ice with a shovel.

Mom posts the
video everywhere.

SAVING THE CITY

I cancel
my meetings.

I cancel
everyone's meetings.

Plows and skid steers
scrape the streets.

The rest of us use
shovels,
hammers, and
crowbars to chop ice.

Even the librarian
kicks
ice with her
high heels.

(Until a firefighter
finds her some boots.)

FLOODING

The first
responders
get called out.

They leave.

Now it's just us office
people
chopping ice.

Wind blows rain and
road salt in my
eyes. The storm siren
wails. I look up.

A pine tree
floats down
Main Street.

Then a baby buggy
swims past.

It looks
unreal.
Like a prank.

It's over, I think.

BREAK

We all
warm up in the
Main Hall.

I fix tea.
Pass around mugs.

Chief Park calls me.
I post her
update in
FaceChat.

Don't step in
floodwaters.

Even a few inches
of fast water
can knock
you down.
Send you
spinning into the
hungry river.

Stay indoors.

EMERGENCY

I refresh
FaceChat.

Listen to the
police scanner.

I want to know what's happening.

My parents are safe.
Pizza, Alex, and Gigi, too.

But all over the
city, people are calling.
People are stuck in
cars. On roofs.
Up trees.

They're calling
911 and
getting a busy signal.

THE CALL

My phone
buzzes. It's
Ruth.

She hasn't
called me since
her stroke.

"Ruth?"

Silence.

I wait.

"Are you okay?"

Silence.

The word comes
slowly. "Underwear."

I know what that means.
Underwater.

I try dispatch again.
I text Chief Park.

But no one can help.

SKYWAY TO THE LIBRARY

"Lisa," I
say. "Give me the
keys to the library."

"Why?"

"Got to get that
book display
started," I say.

"What?"

"The boat. In the
book display.
I'm going to
take her out.
Help people."

"Are you losing your mind?" she asks.

"How can you
lose something
you never had?" I ask.

BACKUP

Alex looks online.
Tells me what
to bring on
a boat rescue.

Lisa gets the safety kit.
Rope ladder.
Flashlight.
First aid.

I find a book.
Smash the glass
firebox.
Take the hammer.

"Now you need something
to test the water depth in
the dark," Alex says.

"Got it,"
Lisa says. "Yardsticks and
glow-in-the-dark craft
stickers."

THE BOOK DISPLAY

I slip on a
life jacket. It has a
stencil.

SAVE OUR FREEDOM TO READ.

We try to move the
boat. It's way too
heavy.

I look out through the
glass lobby doors.
Water is building up on the
street.

"I'll open them," Lisa says.

"The water could
knock you down," I warn.

"Get in the boat," she says.

I do.

LISA OPENS THE DOORS

Water
rushes into the lobby.

It lifts the
boat.

I'm floating.
Spinning.
Racing.

Lisa climbs into the boat
just as it slides
out the door
into the
raging street.

BOATING

I get the motor
started. With
a little power,
I can keep us
steady.

We go slowly.
Pass the
empty Froyo shop.
The tables
float in the
window.

Ahead, somebody's
porch couch
looms like a
hippo in the
water. We
go around it.

I text Ruth:
On our way.
In a boat.

Just then,
Jussie texts.

JUSSIE'S TEXT

*Sarah and I are
stuck on the
roof of her
car,
2343 Green St.*

Water is rising.

*911 is busy.
Help!*

Green Street is
way out by the
marina.

Park Pines is in the
other direction.

Who else has a boat?

Ada,
I forward Jussie's
text to Ada. Add a
boat emoji.

She texts back:
On it.

TURNING DOWN PINE STREET

A red buoy
passes us,
flying in the
current.

"Uh-oh," Lisa
says. "What's that
buoy doing there?
Did the flood
break up the docks?"

I glance back.
A big white
speedboat is
racing toward us.

We steer into
someone's flooded
yard and watch it
pass.

"Yes," I say.
"I think the storm did
break up the docks."

CROSSING PINE CREEK

I shine the flashlight.
The muddy water
writhes. It moves like
angry animals
escaping the zoo.
Someone's white fence
flies by.

"Hold on," I tell
Lisa, and we
steer into it
toward Park Pines.

PARK PINES
NURSING HOME

The power's out.
But red exit lights
glow in the windows.
Shine red on the water.

I use the hammer to
smash open the
glass doors.

Then we row inside,
using the
oars to beat
back floating
tables and
lamps and
walkers.

RUTH

is
sitting on
top of her
dresser.

Water swirls
inches beneath her feet.

We boat close.
I reach for her hand.

Zap!

She buzzed me.

WHAT NEXT

It's hard
to get Ruth in
the boat. She
can't move her
left side.

But we make it.

"How many
more people are here?"
I ask.

Ruth holds up
five fingers.

"Did most people
get out already?"

She nods.

"Our boat
will only
fit two more," I say.

"We'll take two trips," Lisa
says. "Hurry.
The water's rising."

ROWING THROUGH THE HOME

I call out
for Frida,
Gigi's Grandma.

But we find a man instead.
Robert. He's
riding a floating
table.

We find a woman,
Helen, in the
kitchen.

She's perched on a
counter, eating cookies.

"Found the Oreos," she
says. "Guess I'll eat as
many as I want."

Now our boat is full.

WHAT HAPPENS NEXT

We're
motoring
out.

A wall of water
rolls toward us.

There's no escape.
I hold my breath.

The wave
crashes.
Our boat pitches and
spins.

But we stay
afloat. The wave passes.
We're all still here.
All in the boat.

The wave hits
the building. A
window pops.
Water pours in.

THE ROOF

"The roof,"
Lisa says. "If I
could get up there,
I could let
down the
rope ladder.
People could
climb. Then
we could row into the building.
Get the others—"

But these people can't
climb.

Ruth can't use her left
side. Helen's
arm is broken.
Robert shakes too much.

I CLOSE MY EYES

"I'm sorry,
Frida," I whisper.

Is Gigi's grandma
going to die here?

Then,
I hear it.

The slow
glug of
a motor.

A speedboat in
neutral.

A light
shines on
the water.

A voice
cries out,
choked with
fear. "Ivy! Ivy Sawyer!
Are you
okay?"

It's Gretel Griffin.

GRETEL'S BOAT

"Gretel!" I yell.
"Your mom's
still inside."

"This boat won't fit
through the doors.
It's too big!"
Gretel shouts.

We hook the boats
together with the
rope ladder.

We help Ruth and
Robert and Helen
roll across it.

I jump in the water to
steady them.
A current tugs.
My life jacket bobs.
My hands go
numb.

But it works.
Everyone is safe
in Gretel's boat.

SHIVERING IN A SPACE BLANKET

Lisa rows us
back into the building.

The water's so
deep now, I can
touch the red exit sign.

I call out in the
red darkness.

Hello.
We're here.
Frida?

At last we hear
a faint voice.

"In the library."

PARK PINES LIBRARY

I shine the
flashlight.

Lisa rows.

A book
floats by.
Then another.

We follow the
trail of
swimming novels to
the library.

Three women
stand on top of an
upright piano.

One holds a book light.
In its glow, I see
her face.

"Frida," I say,
"It's me. Ivy.
Gigi's friend."

PIANO RESCUE

I climb out of
the boat.

Step into the
water. Onto the
piano keys.

They clank.

I help the women
step down and
into the boat.

When their
toes strike the
piano keys,
tones ring out.

READING

We row through a
field of
open books
floating like lily pads.

Frida holds up her
book light.
Shines it on a
bobbing
paperback.

"I read that one," she
says. She has a thick
Dutch accent.
"There are some real
juicy parts.
You'd like them, Helen.
It's all
love canals and
rock-hard—
oh, is that Gretel
in a speedboat?"

HOSPITAL

They warm us with
blankets. Tea.
Hot IVs. I
fall asleep.

When I wake up,
I see Jussie.

They're lying on
the next cot over.

Their black-violet
eyes meet mine.
But my heart
keeps its even beat.

JUSSIE'S EYES

One look from
Jussie
used to shred
my soul.

Which was good.

Because how else can you
tell you have a soul?

But now
my soul feels
un-shredded.

Maybe I didn't ever need
Jussie.

Maybe I just needed more
uncertainty.

"I'm glad you're okay," I say.

"Yeah. Saved by Big Money,"
Jussie laughs.

"Hey. You lived to fight another day."

100 MESSAGES

The roads are still
flooded.

So is my phone.

Mom sends
Pizza pics. Dad
texts: *So proud.*

Gigi says: *how did
my mom get a
boat?* and
Alex says: *Hey, hero.
Snag a book deal.*

Ada says:
How about that key to the city?

Chief Park updates me
about all the rescues.

But all I care about is this:

EVERYONE LIVED.

HOW GRETEL GOT A BOAT

We drink hospital coffee and she
tells me:

"I drove out to get my mom.
But the road flooded.
I stopped the car and prayed.
A speedboat
floated by. It
got stuck in a fence.
I climbed in.
Hot-wired it. Boom."

"How'd you know how to
hot-wire a boat?" I ask.

"I have my ways."

I look down. "Gretel?
Are you wearing
wooden shoes?"

"They're Dutch.
They're made for floods."

RUTH

Ruth doesn't have
a smartphone.

So I help her
video chat with
her kids.

She points at
Mike's square.
Says, "Femur."

Deb says, "Mom?
Your leg okay?"

Mike says. "Oh!
FEMA! Ivy.
Call City
Hall. Declare an
emergency.
Get the
governor.
Ask for
federal help
for the city."

CLEAN UP

I help Lisa clean the
library lobby. Muddy
water stains the
walls. She
picks up a
soggy book.
Squeezes it.
It drips. "Oh,
this one's got
juicy bits. Have to
give it to Frida," she
jokes.

DR. BRUNO'S BOAT

Principal Bruno
stops by with
bagels.

He says: "My Censor-
Ship held up
pretty well in a
storm, eh?"

"Wait," I say. "That was
your boat? You're on the
Parents' Board?"

"I'm the chair," he says.
"Surprised?"

"Well . . . I thought
you were more of a
ban guy."

"Of course he's not," Lisa says.
"Why do you think he's so
scared of Gretel?
She once followed him
around a Best Buy
for two hours."

THE GOVERNOR

Governor Flores visits.
His feet squeak in
new rubber boots.

He helps
Ken rip out the
wet carpet
in his new apartment.

Reporters watch.
It's all
for show. But
Ken *does* get
new carpet.

Payne serves
Flores a cone of
Flores Ripple. Flores
feeds it to his dog.

But he calls the president.
Tells her we need
money for repairs.

The money comes through.

COUNCIL MEETING

Ruth comes back.
Everyone claps.

Brinda sits next
to her. She's
wearing
Party Pink
lipstick again.

She and
Ruth whisper
so much I have
to bang the
gavel at them.

When the meeting ends
Brinda says,
"We have an idea."

THE ELECTRIC
THIRD RAIL

"We'd like to
touch the third rail,"
Brinda says.
She looks at me and translates:
"That means something
we *never* discuss."

Ruth uses a
pencil to press her
hand buzzer.

It goes zzzzap.

"We did the
math," Brinda says. "If we take
the emergency
money. And
raise parking fees—"

Casey, Ray, and I gasp.

"If we raise
parking fees,
we won't have to
sell our water," Brinda says.

MIKE BOONE, TROLL HUNTER

Mike can be anyone
online. So I ask him
to hunt trolls. At least
till his trial.

So now
if anyone complains about
parking fees,
he says:

*Parking fees are
better than some
punks stealing
your water and
selling it back to you
for $9 a gallon.*

HEADLINES

"Hero Mayor" Survives Recall

Sawyer to Keep Job

*Council Raises
Parking Fees in 4-0 Vote.*

*"Just a Mess, Like All of Us:"
Sawyer Speaks Out About Mike Boone*

*Parking Fee Increase Leads
to Street Brawl*

*River Vale High:
Mayor, Others Graduate*

*Pranks and Rec:
Sawyer to Speak at
U.S. Mayors' Summit*

*Sawyer Attends Young Elected
Leaders Event*

WRITING MY OWN HEADLINES

Mayor and Pup Get
Own Apartment

Mayor's Parents
Seek Therapy

Mayor Goes Gray, Gets
New "Wolf Cut" Hairstyle

State U News: Mayor
Sleeps on Best Friend's Dorm Floor,
Gets Head Stepped On

Mayor Kisses Mayor
at Youth Summit

Wind Farm Windfall?
Mayor Wins Grant for
Renewable Power.

HOMECOMING PARADE

Ruth and I wave on the
parade float. We throw
paper windmills
into the crowd.

Kids made them from
flooded books.

"Wind power? We
got real power," Ruth says.

The words twist her lips.
But she can say them.

Ruth raises both arms,
strong again.

The crowd cheers.

I know what she means.
The real power?
It's us.

WANT TO KEEP READING?

If you liked this book, check out another
book from West 44 Books:

KIKI IN THE MIDDLE
BY ANN MALASPINA

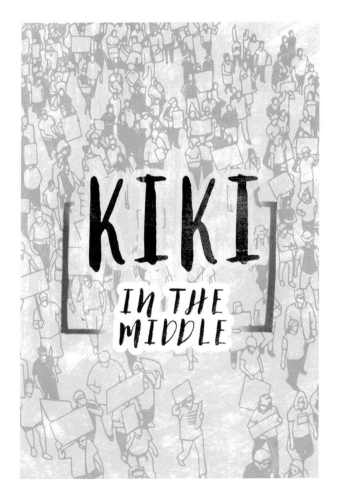

ISBN: 9781978596061

Jones Beach

It's Rami's idea to skip the
second-to-last day of school.

By the time his uncle drops us off in his Uber,
Jones Beach is hot as an oven.

Squeezing
      onto Sonya's old bedspread,
           I already see what I want to draw:

               a herring gull
             with black wing tips
        circling a trash can.

The gull snags a hot dog.
        Sonya and Rami argue about politics.

But before I draw,
I do
what Mamá always told Stavros and me

to never
ever do.

Sun Glare and Salt Water

Eyes shut, I turn my face to the sun.

Spider-web eyelids.
        Fire-orange light.
          Aching color.
            Ouch, my eyes hurt!

Flipping over, I grab my charcoal and sketchbook.

Before I can draw the gull's beak,
     Sonya spills her red slushy on my leg.
       Rami kicks sand in my hair.

Chasing them into the green Atlantic Ocean,
I'm knocked over by the first wave.

I thrash wildly, spitting salt.

       HELP ME! I'M DROWNING!

Like a giant octopus,
     my friends' arms
       encircle me.

They carry me to shore.

Am I an Artist?

The last day of school, Mr. Bevin gives me
the application for 10th grade Honors Art.

Also, the sign-up for Basic Drawing
at the community college this summer.

You need colors in your portfolio, he says.

Is he talking about red slushies, orange suns,
and green oceans?

No, thanks...
Colors aren't...
I'm not that kind of...

He raises his hand, rainbow-stained
from the school paints I never used.

You're not an artist yet, Kiki.

CHECK OUT MORE BOOKS AT:
www.west44books.com

ABOUT THE AUTHOR

Max Howard is the pen name of a poet who wound up becoming a politician. Max's writing for young adults has been recognized by the Junior Library Guild, the American Library Association, and Maine's North Star Award committee. Max is the author of *Fifteen and Change*, *The Water Year*, *Surviving American History*, and *Everything in Its Path*.